NO ZOMBIES ALLOWED

by Matt Novak

A Richard Jackson Book

Atheneum Books for Young Readers

New York London Toronto Sydney Singapore

Atheneum Books for Young Readers
An imprint of Simon & Schuster Children's Publishing Division
1230 Avenue of the Americas
New York, New York 10020

Book design by Sonia Chaghatzbanian
The text of this book is set in Alcoholica.
The illustrations are rendered in watercolor.

Printed in Hong Kong
First Edition

10 9 8 7 6 5 4 3 2 1

Library of Congress Cataloging-in-Publication Data
Novak, Matt.
No zombies allowed / by Matt Novak.—1st ed.
p. cm.

"A Richard Jackson book."

Summary: As they look at photographs of their previous year's Monster
Party, two witches begin to exclude zombies, ghosts, and vampires to
avoid problems, but finally decide that a party is more fun when everyone
is included.

ISBN 0-689-84130-2

[1. Witches—Fiction. 2. Parties—Fiction. 3. Halloween—Fiction.] I. Title.
PZ7.N867 No 2001
[E]—dc21   00-037125

Dedicated to frustrated
party planners everywhere

MONSTER
PARTY
TONIGHT

Witch Wizzle and Witch Woddle were getting ready
for their annual monster party.

"Where are the ghoulish games and the monstrous music?"
asked Witch Wizzle.

"I don't remember," sighed Witch Woddle. "I can't find
anything in this messy house."

"We should do some cleaning," said Witch Wizzle.

Wizzle picked up a box and something fell out.
"Oh look!" she cried. "I found a photo
from our party last year."
"Let me see," said Woddle.

"I remember this now," said Wizzle. "Those zombies kept dropping their eyes into the punch bowl."

"And they never talked," Woddle said. "They just sat there like, well, zombies. They practically ruined the party."

"We should be more careful about who we allow in this year," said Wizzle.

So Wizzle and Woddle made a big sign
and put it in front of their house.

"That should keep them away," said Woddle.
"This will be the biggest and best party
we ever had."

Behind the sofa they found another photo. "Werewolves," said Wizzle. "Remember how they coughed up furballs all over the house, and how their howls shattered the windows?"
"I am still finding fleas in the furniture," said Woddle. "Werewolves are worse than zombies."

And they put an even bigger sign out in their yard.

"Now everyone who comes will enjoy the party," said Wizzle.

NO WEREWOLVES ALLOWED

There were photos in the refrigerator.

"How did they get in there?" asked Wizzle.

"I don't remember," said Woddle, "but I do remember that those swamp creatures tracked slime all through the house."

"And they just would not come out of the bathroom all night," said Wizzle. "We don't want any swamp creatures in our house this year."

They added yet another sign to their yard. "Parties sure are hard work," grunted Wizzle.

Woddle rolled up the carpet.
"Uh-oh," she said. More photos. "I almost forgot
about the ghosts, the skeletons, and the vampires."
"Yes," said Wizzle. "Those ghosts moaned and groaned
about everything, the skeletons kept calling everyone Fatso,
and the vampires sucked all the juice out of the fruit.
We have to keep them all out."

"Absolutely," Woddle agreed.

"That should take care of all of our problems," said Woddle, as they pounded the biggest sign of all into the ground.

"We better see if there are any more photos," Wizzle said.

There were photos under the sink,

on top of the bookshelf,

and inside the piano.

"My goodness!" exclaimed Woddle. "We almost overlooked all those witches who came last year. Remember how their brooms knocked everything over, and how their pointy hats kept poking everyone in the eyes?"

"I do remember," Wizzle said. "They sprinkled love potion all over the snake snacks and flew around turning everyone into frogs. Witches are the worst of all."

"Right," said Woddle. "We won't allow any witches."

"Wait a minute," said Witch Wizzle. "Isn't this you?"

"And isn't this you?" asked Witch Woddle.

"Now that I think about it," said Wizzle,
"that wasn't such a bad party."
"It really was a lot of fun," said Woddle.

They took down all the signs.

"There is just one more sign we need to make," Wizzle said.
"I know just what you mean," said Woddle.

And Wizzle and Woddle's party
was the biggest and best there ever was.

At least, that's how they remembered it.